William Malone Baskervill

Irwin Russell

ISBN/EAN: 9783337170905

Printed in Europe, USA, Canada, Australia, Japan

Cover: Foto ©Raphael Reischuk / pixelio.de

More available books at **www.hansebooks.com**

William Malone Baskervill

Irwin Russell

No. 3. Ten Cents.   Per Year, One Dollar.

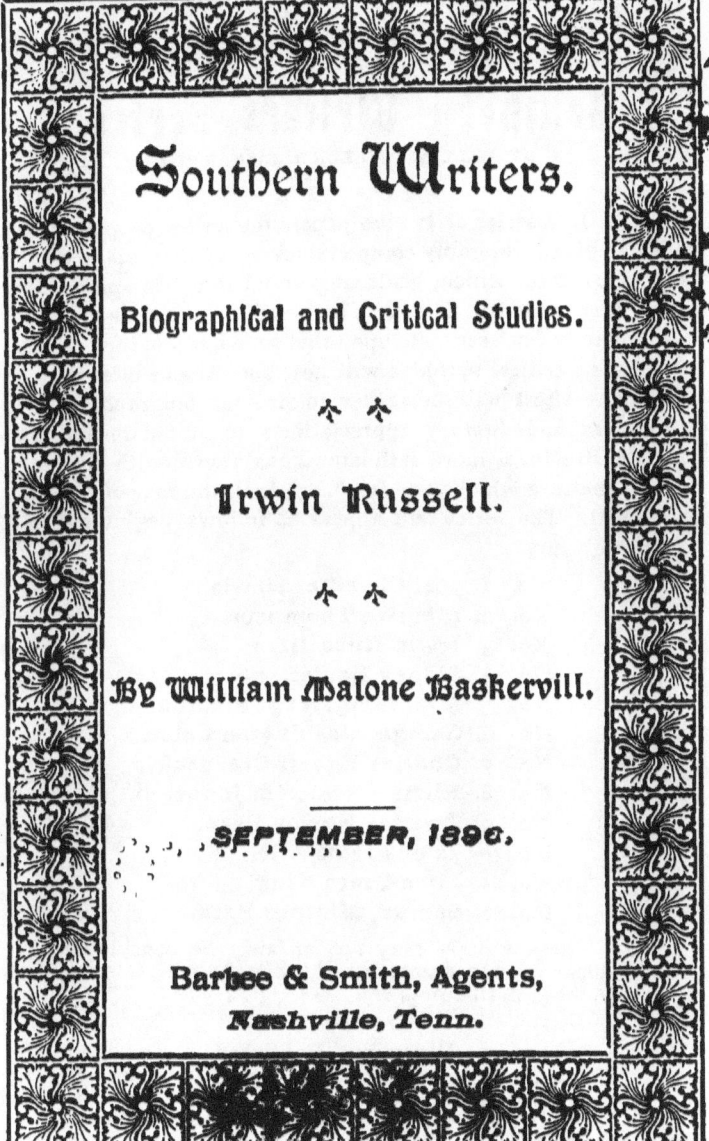

Southern Writers.

Biographical and Critical Studies.

✦ ✦

Irwin Russell.

✦ ✦

By William Malone Baskervill.

————

SEPTEMBER, 1896.

Barbee & Smith, Agents,
Nashville, Tenn.

7/5)0

Southern Writers Series.

BY WILLIAM MALONE BASKERVILL.

IN a series of twelve papers the writer proposes to give a tolerably complete survey of that literary movement which, beginning about 1870, has spread over the entire South. There will be no attempt to place a final estimate upon this contribution, though some critical opinions will now and then be offered. The effort will be rather to present biographical *data* and literary appreciations—to stimulate the desire for a more intimate acquaintance with this literature which is so fresh, original, and racy of the soil. The series will appear as follows, beginning with July:

No. 1. Joel Chandler Harris.
No. 2. Maurice Thompson.
No. 3. Irwin Russell.
No. 4. Sidney Lanier.
No. 5. Mrs. Margaret J. Preston.
No. 6. George Washington Cable.
No. 7. Charles Egbert Craddock.
No. 8. Richard Malcolm Johnston.
No. 9. Thomas Nelson Page.
No. 10. James Lane Allen.
No. 11. Miss Grace King.
No. 12. Samuel Minturn Peck.

These writers may not unfairly be considered typical and representative of the best that has been produced in this new era.

SOUTHERN WRITERS: Published Monthly. Subscription price, $1 a year. Single copies, 10 cents, postage paid.

Send orders for the whole series or for separate numbers to

BARBEE & SMITH, Agents,

Nashville, Tenn.

Irwin Russell.

A YOUNG Marylander, a stripling just from college, was dreaming dreams from which he was awakened by the guns of Sumter. One sleepless night in April, 1861, he wrote the poem, " My Maryland," which may not inaptly be called the first note of the new Southern literature—" new in strength, new in depth, new in the largest elements of beauty and truth." He that had ears to hear might have heard in the booming of those guns not only the signal for a gigantic contest, but also the proclamation of the passing away of the old order, and along with it the wax-flowery, amateurish, and sentimental race of Southern writers.

But first should come the terrible experiences of a mighty conflict, in which the soul of the people was to be brought out through struggles,

passions, partings, heroism, love,
death—all effective in the production
of genuine feeling and the develop-
ment of real character. While the
battles were being fought in the
homes of the Southerners, their
poets sent forth, now a stirring,
martial lyric, now a humorous song
or poem recounting the trials and
hardships of camp, hospital, and
prison life, these becoming ever
more and more intermingled with
dirges—for Jackson, for Albert Sidney Johnston, for Stuart, for Ashby,
and finally for the " Conquered Ban-
ner." But in all of these there was
no trace of artificiality, no sign of
mawkish sentimentality. They were
surcharged with deep, genuine, sin-
cere feeling ; they were instinct with
life. In this respect the war poetry
laid the foundation for the new literature.

Accompanying the return to reality was a social earthquake which
laid bare the rich literary deposits in

which the South abounded. As one
of the best of the new school has
said, "Never in the history of this
country has there been a generation
of writers who came into such an
inheritance of material as has fallen
to these younger writers of the
South." Under the new order
Southern life and manners were for
the first time open to a full and free
report and criticism.

It is noticeable that in the racy,
humorous writings of Longstreet,
Thompson, Meek, and others—
sketches which contained the elements of real life—the negro is con-
spicuous for his absence. At that
time there was enough and to spare
written about him by way of defense,
vindication, or apology, but to use
him as art material seemed to be far
from the thoughts of Southern writers. The only notable book in which
negro character was made use of
chanced to be a phenomenal success;
but as it was written on the principle

of antagonism, and as it really served as the signal for the deadly struggle which followed, it was altogether natural that Southern writers would not imitate this example. After the war, however, the one subject which hitherto could have been treated with least freedom became the most prolific theme of the new writers. Consciously or unconsciously, they one and all, with one noteworthy exception, adopted a method diametrically opposed to that of the author of " Uncle Tom's Cabin." They were either those whose lives had been purified in the fires of adversity and defeat, or buoyant, ardent young souls " with the freshness of early dew upon their wings."

This literature of the new South had for its cardinal principles good will and sympathy. Its aims were to cement bonds of good fellowship between the sections, to depict the negro according to his real character, and to exhibit to the world the true relations which existed between master and slave.

Irwin Russell was among the first, if not the very first, of Southern writers to appreciate the literary possibilities of the negro character and of the unique relations existing between the two races before the war, and was among the first to develop them, says Joel Chandler Harris. This skillful delineator of unique and peculiar character was naturally drawn to the sensitive, erratic, but exquisitely attuned young poet, and he contributed the "Introduction" when his slender remnant was published in 1888 by the Century Company under the title: "Poems by Irwin Russell." The whole story is told in a few simple words by Mr. Harris, in which he says of Russell: "He possessed in a remarkable degree what has been described as the poetical temperament, and though he was little more than twenty-six years old at the time of his death, his sufferings and his sorrows made his life a long one. He had at his command everything that affection could suggest; he had loyal friends wherever he went; but in spite of all this, the waywardness of genius led continually in the direction of suffering and sorrow. In the rush and hurly-burly of the practical, everyday world he found himself helpless; and so, after a brief struggle, he died."

It is surprising how few in the South know anything of this young poet except his name, and many have never heard that. Only one sketch of him has found its way into the literary journals, and that is a very interesting and valuable paper in the *Critic*, written by Charles C. Marble, who seems to have had a close personal acquaintance with the "unhappy boy." Another paper of still more vividly personal interest was written by Catherine Cole and published in the *New Orleans Times-*

Democrat. But for much of the personal matter the writer is indebted to the young poet's mother, who, though an invalid, is still living.

In Irwin Russell's veins mingled the blood of Virginia and of New England. His paternal great-grandfather was a soldier of the Revolution, and hailed from the Old Dominion. His grandfather was born and reared in this state, but after reaching manhood he went thence to Ohio, where he settled and married a woman of fine intellect, a native of the Isle of Wight, Miss Mary McNab. One of their sons is still living, Mr. Addison P. Russell, who was formerly Secretary of State in Ohio, but is better known now as the author of several books: "Library Notes," "A Club of One," and "In a Club Corner." Irwin's father, Dr. William McNab Russell, grew up in Ohio, studied medicine, and was married to a young lady, a native of New York, but of New

England ancestry. The newly married pair then sought a home in Mississippi, settling at Port Gibson, where the young doctor engaged in the practice of medicine, becoming in a short time very successful. Here it was, June 3, 1853—the year in which the author of "Marse Chan" first saw the light in Virginia—that Irwin Russell was born. Almost immediately, at three months of age, he was subjected to an attack of yellow fever, which terrible scourge was then raging as an epidemic. That same year the family and home were transferred to St. Louis, Mo., where they remained until the breaking out of the Civil War. Then Dr. Russell took his family back to Port Gibson to cast in his lot with the Confederacy; for, like almost every Northerner that had made his home in the South, he was an ardent sympathizer with this section.

While at St. Louis Irwin was

placed in school, for he was a re-
markably precocious boy, having
learned to read well at four years of
age. He was a diligent little stu-
dent, and so general was his infor-
mation that his young friends used
to call him the "walking cyclopedia."
Again, after the war, he was sent
back to this city to be placed in the
St. Louis University, which was
under the charge of the Jesuit fathers, and from which he was grad-
uated in 1869 with high credit. At
college he kept up his studious habits and gave evidence of real ability,
his talents being more particularly
shown in the line of higher mathe-
matics. Mr. Marble writes: "I remember hearing him talk brilliant-
ly of the science of navigation, of
which, theoretically, he was master.
He had discovered a method of ex-
actly ascertaining the latitude from
observations of the sun's altitude
and deviation from the meridian;
and when it was favorably reported

upon by certain scientific persons he immediately applied to the captain of a ship for the privilege of making a voyage with him, that he might test and increase his knowledge of navigation."

After graduation he returned to Mississippi, read law, and by a special act of the Legislature he was admitted to the bar at the age of nineteen. He practiced for awhile, and became specially proficient in conveyancing, which is said to require very exact technical knowledge. But one of his peculiar tastes and disposition could hardly be expected to confine himself to the daily routine and drudgery of a law office. He was inclined to diversions; one, for example, was the printer's trade, which he learned so thoroughly as to become a dainty compositor, and in time he grew to be critically fond of old prints and black-letter volumes — a real connoisseur, recognizing at a glance

the various types used in book-
making. He delighted to pick up
odd volumes of the old dramatists,
and took special pride in possessing
one of the oldest copies of Wycher-
ly in existence. He was also given
to roving; and, like Robert Louis
Stevenson, he might have been
known and pointed out for the pattern of an idler. Once, when under
the spell which Captain Marryatt
not infrequently has thrown over a
romantic and impulsive youth, he
left home, Mr. Marble tells us,
much to the discomfort of his par-
ents, and lived in a sailors' boarding
house in New Orleans. While
there he habitually dressed as a
sailor, and one day he applied for
a position to a captain about to sail
to the Mediterranean. "Abandon-
ing for the time being," continues
Mr. Marble, " his spectacles (which,
as he had when he was only two
years old lost the sight of one eye
by the stab of a penknife which

he unfortunately found lying open, and was nearsighted in the other, was a serious matter), he rowed out alongside the ship and with the greatest difficulty got on board. He was examined, of course, minutely and critically by the first mate, and told to come the next day. But he saw the probability of long and hard service, and abandoned the notion of thus seeing life, even if he could have succeeded in concealing his blindness till the ship sailed. But the sea never ceased to have " a perpetual fascination for him."

Fields for observation and for the study of character were thus offered to his inner eye, however much the outer ones were shut in by blindness and nearsightedness. The grotesque appealed to him strongly, and as he had acquired facility in drawing, he made numerous and fantastic sketches on scraps of paper, old envelopes, or whatever was at hand, as material for future use. His skill in caricature reminded his friends not a little of Thackeray. Love of nature was in him a passion; and a splendid sunset, a gorgeous Southern forest, or other natural scenes, he keenly enjoyed and beautifully described. Mr. Marble says: "He saw every bird, took note of every strange conformation of nature, was familiar with the names of trees and plants, had an eye for prospects, an ear for sound, an exquisite sensitiveness for nature's perfume, and a rollicking enjoyment of the country." He was also very fond of music, played the piano well, and was an expert on the banjo. His talents were versatile, and in him was found the exquisite delicacy of organism so frequently seen in modern poets, which vibrated to every appeal. He was sensitive alike to internal and external impressions, changes of weather or temperature, grotesque or humorous characters, different manners and tongues, and particularly responsive to the influences of the great masters of fiction and poetry.

At some time or other Irwin Russell must have had a rarely sympathetic companion or guide in literary study. Was it one of the Jesuit fathers, or his own father, " who was idolized by the son?" We know not. But his extreme nicety in the use of language, his quick and retentive ear for dialect, his ability to imitate almost perfectly the poets, and his deep reading in literature for one of his age were all remarkable and gave evidence of careful training and study. He was another example of that rare union of bright mind with frail body through which the keenest appreciation and the most exquisite sensibility are developed.

At times, too, he was capable of painstaking application and ardent devotion to study. He made a

110

close study of Chaucer and "Percy's Reliques," and the old English dramatists were his constant companions, the sources of never-failing enjoyment. He caught the tones of Herrick or Thackeray's ballads with equal ease; greatly admired Byron, and was powerfully influenced by Shelley. In his correspondence there was here an echo of Carlyle, there of Thackeray or some other master. Though his reading was confined mainly to English literature, he knew Molière's dramas, even wishing to translate "Tartufe" and "Le Misanthrope," and took the keenest delight in Rabelais, whose wit, sarcasm, and satiric exaggeration he longed to apply to the follies and deformities of more modern life. "The margins of his copy of this author," says a friend, "and many interleaved pages were filled with notes and comments; and William Dove himself, whom Southey describes as a ' practical Pantagruelist,' was not more influenced by his pages. He literally, as he somewhere says, had the best parts of Rabelais by heart."

But his chief favorite was Burns, whose influences are everywhere visible. " Christmas Night in the Quarters " reminds us strongly now of the "Jolly Beggars," now of " Tam O'Shanter." His imitation of Burns's " Epistles " is so perfect that we could easily believe that the Scottish bard wrote the following stanzas :

The warld, they say, is gettin' auld;
Yet in her bosom, I've been tauld,
A burnin', youthfu' heart's installed—
    I dinna ken—
But sure her face seems freezin' cauld
    To some puir men.

In summer, though the sun may shine,
Aye still the winter's cauld is mine--
But what o' that? The manly pine
    Endures the storm!
Ae spark o' Poesy divine
    Will keep me warm.

112

In almost boyish abandon he says: "Burns is my idol. He seems to me the greatest man that ever God created, beside whom all other poets are utterly insignificant. In fact, my feelings in this regard are precisely equivalent to those of the old Scotchman mentioned in 'Library Notes,' who was consoled in the hour of death by the thought that he should see Burns."

For the writing of negro dialect and the delineation of negro character Irwin Russell had the gift of genius and all the advantages of opportunity. As he himself said: "I have lived long among the negroes (as also long enough away from them to appreciate their peculiarities); understand their character, disposition, language, customs, and habits; have studied them, and have them continually before me." But with him dialect was a second consideration. He used it as Shakespeare did in "King Lear,"

as Fielding did in "Joseph An-
drews," as Scott, Thackeray,
George Eliot, and all the great
masters have used it—as the only
natural medium for the presenta-
tion of certain kinds of character.
In another garb they would be mas-
querading. As the author of "Uncle Remus" has aptly said, "The
dialect is not always the best—it is
often carelessly written—but the
negro is there, the old-fashioned,
unadulterated negro, who is still
dear to the Southern heart. There
is no straining after effect—indeed,
the poems produce their result by
indirection; but I do not know
where could be found to-day a hap-
pier or a more perfect representa-
tion of negro character."

Not the least important of the
shaping influences which contributed to this result is sympathetically
suggested by "One Mourner," in
"Befo' de War," "Whar's sorry
Marse Irwin's dead:"

He couldn' 'a' talked so nachal
   'Bout niggers in sorrow and joy,
Widdouten he had a black mammy
   To sing to him 'long ez a boy.

But his chief title to our consideration is originality. As Mr. Page has said, "He laid bare a lead in which others have since discovered further treasures." Like many another original discovery, this was made in a very simple, natural way. To a friend who asked him how he came to write in negro dialect, he answered: "It was almost an inspiration. I did not reduce the trifle to writing until some time afterwards, and then, from want of recollection, in a much condensed and emasculated form. You know that I am something of a banjoist. Well, one evening I was sitting in our back yard in old Mississippi, 'twanging' on the banjo, when I heard the missis—our colored domestic, an old darky of the Aunt Dinah pattern—singing one of the

outlandish camp meeting hymns of
which the race is so fond. She was
an extremely 'ligious character and,
although seized with the impulse to
do so, I hesitated to take up the
tune and finish it. I did so, however, and in the dialect that I have
adopted, and which I then thought,
and still think, is in strict conformity
to their use of it, I proceeded, as
one inspired, to compose verse after
verse of the most absurd, extrava-
gant, and, to her, irreverent rhyme
ever before invented, all the while
accompanying it on the banjo, and
imitating the fashion of the planta-
tion negro. The old missis was so
exasperated and indignant that she
predicted all sorts of dire calamities.
Meantime my enjoyment of it was
prodigious. I was then about sixteen, and as I had soon after a like
inclination to versify, was myself
pleased with the performance, and
it was accepted by the publisher, I
have continued to work the vein in-

definitely. There is much in it, such as it is."

Russell's appreciation of the darky was wonderful. The negro's humor and his wisdom were a constant marvel to him. What would strike an ordinary observer as merely ludicrous glistened by the reflected light of his mind like a proverb. The darky's insight into human nature and circumstances he believed to be more than instinct: such infallible results could only come from deduction. When asked whether there was any real poetry in the negro character, he replied: " Many think the vein a limited one, but I tell you that it is inexhaustible. The Southern negro has only just so much civilization as his contact with the white man has given him, He has only been indirectly influenced by the discoveries of science, the inventions of human ingenuity, and the general progress of mankind. Without education or social inter-

course with intelligent and cultivated
people, his thought has necessarily
been original. . . . He has not
been controlled in his convictions by
historic precedent, and yet he has
often manifested a foresight and
wisdom in practical matters worthy
of the higher races. You may call
it instinct, imitation, what you will;
it has, nevertheless, a foundation. I
am a Democrat, was a Rebel, but I
have long felt that the negro, even
in his submission and servitude, was
conscious of a higher nature, and
must some day assert it. . . .
I have felt that the soul could not be
bound, and must find a way for it-
self to freedom. The negro race,
too, in spite of oppression, has re-
tained qualities found in few others
under like circumstances. Grati-
tude it has always been distin-
guished for; hospitality and help-
fulness are its natural creed; brutal-
ity, considering the prodigious depth
of its degradation, is unusual. It

does not lack courage, industry, self-denial, or virtue. . . . So the negro has done an immense amount of quiet thinking; and with only such forms of expression as his circumstances furnished him he indulges in paradox, hyperbole, aphorism, sententious comparison. He treasures his traditions; he is enthusiastic, patient, long-suffering, religious, reverent. Is there not poetry in the character?"

The "Poems" contain for the most part a picture of the negro himself. But only once is he in a reminiscential vein, when we catch a glimpse of the old-time prosperous planter, "Mahsr John," who "shorely wuz the greates' man de country ebber growed:"

I only has to shet my eyes, an' den it
    seems to me
I sees him right afore me now, jes like
    he use' to be,
A settin' on de gal'ry, lookin' awful big
    an' wise,

Wid little niggers fannin' him to keep
    away de flies.
He alluz wore de berry bes' ob planter's
    linen suits,
An' kep' a nigger busy jes a blackin' ob
    his boots,
De buckles on his galluses wuz made ob
    solid gol',
An di'mons! dey was in his shut as thick
    as it would hol'.

There is a slight touch of pathos in

He had to pay his debts, an' so his lan' is
    mos'ly gone,
An' I declar' I's sorry fur my pore ol'
    Mahsr John,

but it does not prevent him from
hiding " rocks " in the bale of cotton
which, in another poem, he endeav-
ors to sell to " Mahsr Johnny."
In general the poems rather give
true presentments of the negro's
queer superstitions and still queerer
ignorances; his fondness for a story,
especially an animal tale or a ghost
story; his habit of talking to himself or the animal that he is plowing
or driving; his gift in prayer and

·shrewd preachments; his love of music, especially on the fiddle and the banjo, and the happy abandonment of his revels; his irresponsible life, his slippery shifts, his injured innocence when discovered—over all of which are thrown the mantle of charity and the mellowing rays of humor and wisdom. Occasionally we chance upon a dainty bit of poetry, as in the verse:

An' folks don't 'spise de vi'let flower bekase it ain't de rose.

But oftener it is practical, homespun wit, in which "Christmas Night in the Quarters," the best delineation of some phases of negro life yet written, specially abounds. Now it is old Jim talking to a slow ox:

Mus' be you think I's dead,
    An' dis de huss you's draggin';
You's mos' too lazy to draw yo' bref,
    Let 'lone drawin' de waggin.

Then Brudder Brown, with native simplicity, proceeds "to beg a blessin' on dis dance:"

Irwin Russell.

Oh Mahsr! let dis gath'rin' fin' a blessin'
   in yo' sight!
Don't jedge us hard fur what we does—
   you know it's Christmus night.

. . . .

You bless us, please, Sah, eben ef we's
   doin' wrong to-night;
'Kase den we'll need de blessin' more'n
   ef we's doin' right.

The dance begins—and a more natural scene than the fiddler "callin' de figgers" was never penned—in which "Georgy Sam" carries off the palm.

      De nigger mus' be, fur a fac',
      Own cousin to a jumpin' jack!

"An tell you what, de *supper* wuz a 'tic'lar sarcumstance," the poet himself not even attempting to describe this scene. But the fun reaches its height when the banjo is called for, and the story of its origin is told: how Ham invented it " fur to amuse hese'f " in the ark. Did Burns ever sing a more rollicking strain than this?

He strung her, tuned her, struck a jig—
  'twas " Nebber Min' de Wedder "—
She soun' like forty-lebben bands a play-
  in' all togedder;
Some went to pattin', some to dancin';
  Noah called de figgers,
An' Ham he sot an' knocked de tune, de
  happiest ob niggers!

So wears the night, and wears so fast,
All wonder when they find it past,
And hear the signal sound to go
From what few cocks are left to crow.

The picture of the freedman is
strikingly characteristic and true to
life. The false sample of cotton
and the hidden stones in the bale
being detected, he is, as usual, ready
enough with an excuse:

Mahsr Johnny, dis is fine.
I's gone and hauled my brudder's cotton
  in, instead ob mine.

He is a great flatterer and has a
" slick tongue," either in begging a
piece of tobacco or in wheedling
" young marster " out of a dollar
for a pup not " wuf de powder it'd

take to blow him up." His pro-
pensity for chickens is notorious;

An' ef a man cain't borry what's layin'
out ob nights,
I'd like you fur to tell me what's de good
of *swivel rights?*

He thinks you "turn State's eb-
bydence" with a crank, and "dem
folks in de Norf is de beatin'est lot!"
In spite of their blue coats and brass
buttons—

I seed 'em de time 'at Grant's army come
froo—

his opinion is:

Dey's ign'ant as ign'ant kin be.
Dey wudn't know gumbo, ef put in dey
mouf—
Why don't dey all sell out an' come to
de Souf?

The negro's insight, observation,
and sententiousness are revealed
through many homely but inimitable aphorisms:

But ef you quits a workin' ebbery time
de sun is hot,
De sheriff's goin' to lebby upon ebbery-
t'ing you's got.

124

I nebber breaks a colt afore he's old
enough to trabbel;
I nebber digs my taters tell dey's plenty
big to grabble.
I don't keer how my apple looks, but
on'y how it tas'es.
De man what keeps pullin' de grapevine
shakes down a few bunches at leas'.
A violeen is like an 'ooman, mighty hard
to guide.

. . . .

Dere's alluz somefin' 'bout it out ob kel-
ter, more or less,
An' tain't de fancies'-lookin' ones dat
alluz does de best.
You nebber heerd a braggin' fiddler
play a decent jig.

There is a touch of sentiment in
the father's parting precepts to his
son, about to seek his fortune as
waiter upon the " Robbut E. Lee : "

It's hard on your mudder, your leabin'—I
don' know whatebber she'll do;
An' shorely your fader'll miss you—I'll
alluz be thinkin' ob you.

But he quickly veils it under true
humor and homely wisdom :

Don't you nebber come back, sah, widout
you has money an' clo'es,

I's kep' you as long as I's gwine to, an'
   now you an' me we is done,
An' calves is too skace in dis country
   to kill for a prodigal son.

All these pictures are perfectly truthful, but as the lawyers say, they are not the whole truth. Perhaps Russell died too young to sound the depths of the negro's emotional nature. He caught no tones like those echoing in Harris's " Bless God, he died free!" or James Whitcomb Riley's wail of the old mother over her dead " Gladness," her only freeborn child.

The last two years of Russell's life present the strange contrasts so often met with in poetical temperaments when the earthborn and the celestial have not been brought into perfect harmony. Acts of nobility and self-sacrifice were quickly followed by thoughtless follies which laid him low. During the whole of the yellow fever epidemic in 1878 he remained in Port Gibson and served as a devoted nurse, though he never escaped from the scenes through which he passed. The ghastly picture haunted his imagination. Two letters written to a friend at the time lift the curtain upon this terrible tragedy of human suffering and helplessness to which he was so nobly ministering.

September 1, 1878, he writes: "All of us are well worn out, nursing; yet we cannot nurse the sick properly, there are so many of them, and many die for want of attention. It is horrible here, you cannot conceive how horrible. Of all who have died here, not one has had any sort of funeral. Rich or poor, there is no difference. As soon as the breath leaves them they are boxed up in pine coffins and buried without the least ceremony of any kind, and nobody to follow them to the grave."

And again on the 30th: "I am worn out from nursing night and day, and performing such other duties as were mine as a 'Howard,' and simply as a man. Four days ago I, for the first time in a month, sat down to a regularly cooked and served meal. I have been living, like Dr. Wango Tango of nursery fame, 'on a biscuit a day,' when I could get it. Happily the epidemic is nearly over in town for want of material. Between six hundred and seven hundred people (out of sixteen hundred) remained in town to face the fever. Out of these there have been about five hundred and seventy cases and one hundred and eighteen deaths up to this date. I will not attempt to give you an idea of the awful horrors I have seen, among which I have lived for the past five or six weeks, besides which I have seen or heard nothing whatever. Hendrik Conscience, Boccaccio, and DeFoe tried to describe similar scenes, and I now realize how utterly they failed. No description can convey a tithe of the reality."

To crown Irwin's misfortunes, his father, whom he idolized and " who had exhausted himself in philanthropic efforts to arrest the scourge," suddenly died. Finely endowed as he was, and developing in very early life a taste for nothing so much as literature, he resisted the efforts of his family to find for him a place in a commercial or monotonous, commonplace calling. Now thrown entirely upon himself, he endeavored to take up life in a manly, courageous way, and set out with many valuable pieces in his literary knapsack for New York City, with the purpose of devoting himself to letters. Here, as everywhere, he found good friends and true, especially Mr. H. C. Bunner, Mr. R. W. Gilder, and Mr. R. U. Johnson, of *Scribner's Monthly*, and others ; and the love, tenderness, and comprehending sympathy with which these men gathered about the boy, trying to shield him from his own weakness, must have been inexpressibly sweet to him, as it is gratefully treasured by his mother to this day, "although I knew," as he said to a friend with boyish sob, "that I would win, not they." He had exhausted all his funds, but shrank from the thought of again calling upon those who had so often befriended him, when he was taken ill of a fever. Mr. Bunner and Mr. Johnson cared for and nursed him, and during the slow days of his convalescence, his head still seriously affected, he could remember nothing of the time but " the mad wish to run away "—from himself, which he had before attempted. So, dazed in mind, he wandered down to the docks and upon the decks of the " Knickerbocker," where he begged to be allowed to work his way to New Orleans. " Gaunt and weak and wretched as I was, they took me," said he, telling his sad story to "Catherine Cole," "and I did a coal heaver and fireman's duty almost all the way down. Landed here, I had no money, no friends, no clothes. I was as black as an imp of Satan, and had a very devil of despair in my heart. I wrote out some stuff—an account of the trip, I believe—and signing my own name to it, took it to the office of the *New Orleans Times.* The city editor, Maj. Robinson, took my copy, looked me over as if he wondered how such a dirty wretch ever got hold of it, and asked me how I came by it. I told him that I had traveled south on the ship with Mr. Russell, and that he had sent me. 'Go back and tell Mr. Russell that I would be pleased to see him,' said the Major, and I did so. I could not present myself again at the *Times* office, so I left a letter there, telling the whole truth, and winding up thus: 'What a time I had in that den of a fireman's forecastle, living on tainted meat and genuine Mark Twain "slum-gullion," I won't try to tell you. I only tell you all this to make you understand why I did not let you know I was my own messenger last night. I never was in such a state before in all my life, and was ashamed to make myself known. However, needs must when the devil drives. I suppose I am not the only sufferer from Panurge's disease, lack o' money, but it is hard to smoke the pipe of contentment when you can't get tobacco.'"

From this time till he died Irwin Russell was a semi-attaché of the *Times* staff, and Mrs. Fields ("Catherine Cole"), who was in charge of the "All Sorts" column, tells how he came daily into her den to scratch off a rhyme or two in inimitable style, adding: "He was gentle and genial, a fellow of infinite jest, and it was no wonder he made loyal friends wherever he went." But he

was now absolutely without hope. "I have always known it," he would say to her, "with a sort of second sight and a premonition of these days, for I believe these are my last days. I feel now, so old am I, as if I could not remember the age when occasionally the desire for some unnatural stimulant did not possess me with a fury of desire. This has been stronger than ambition, stronger than love. I have stretched my moral nature like a boy playing with a piece of elastic, knowing I should snap it presently.
. . . It has been the romance of a weak young man threaded in with the pure love of a mother, a beautiful girl who hoped to be my wife, and friends who believed in my future. I have watched them lose heart, lose faith, and again and again I have been so stung and startled that I resolved to save myself in spite of myself. . . . I never shall."

133

Only a few days after one of these conversations this same friend and others went with their little wreaths of Christmas flowers down into the heart of Franklin Street, a wretched, noisy, dirty neighborhood, and into a forlorn little house, set right upon the street, on whose small wooden shutters hung a bow with floating ends of white tarlatan pinched out rudely at the edges. Children, barefooted and ragged, played in the dusty street; curious, careless passers-by, to whom the youth was all unknown, stopped at the sign of the white bow, and entered in to gaze with ghoulish curiosity upon the stilled form. A policeman stood at the head of the casket, and near by was a faded, sad-eyed little woman, who held out a bundle of letters, the last he had received from his mother and sweetheart. This poor Irish woman living here with her three children rented him a room and cooked his

simple meals. He was a veritable
stranger to her. His only claim on
her was the pittance he paid for
food and lodging. But for divine
charity's sake she had watched
him through the last hours of his
sad life. Hers were the steady
arms that held him when delirium
seized him; hers were the hands
that administered medicine and food;
her time and her sympathy were
freely given; and when at midnight
he died, on a poor cot, in a poor
room up under the roof, her prayers
were the white wings of the guard-
ian angel that accompanied the de-
parting soul through the valley of
the shadow of death.

"Ah! if we pity the good and
weak man who suffers undeserved-
ly, let us deal very gently with him
from whom misery extorts not only
tears, but shame; let us think hum-
bly and charitably of the human nature that suffers so sadly and falls
so low. Whose turn may it be to-

morrow? What weak heart, confident before trial, may not succumb under temptation invincible? Cover the good man who has been vanquished; cover his face and pass on." His remains were first laid away in New Orleans, but subsequently removed to St. Louis, to be placed by the side of his father's, so that even the pious wish of "One Mourner" was denied him.

An' I hopes dey lay him to sleep, seh,
　Somewhar' whar' de birds will sing
About him de livelong day, seh,
　An' de flowers will bloom in spring.

But he still lives as the "Southern humorist," his pitiful story softens our hearts and his blithe spirit sweetens and refreshes our lives.

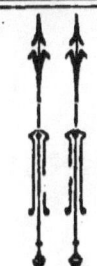

www.ingramcontent.com/pod-product-compliance
Lightning Source LLC
Chambersburg PA
CBHW030910260626
47169CB00008B/2770